Yamamoto

THE CRANE GIRL

BY
VERONIKA MARTENOVA CHARLES

ORCHARD BOOKS
New York

Text and illustrations © Veronika Martenova Charles, 1992
First American Edition 1993 published by Orchard Books.
First published in Canada in 1992 by Oxford University Press.

Orchard Books
95 Madison Avenue
New York, NY 10016

Printed in Hong Kong
Book design by Kathryn Cole and Veronika Martenova Charles

10 9 8 7 6 5 4 3 2 1

Library of Congress Cataloging-in-Publication Data
Charles, Veronika Martenova.
The crane girl / by Veronika Martenova Charles —
1st American ed. p. cm.
Summary: Feeling that the arrival of a new baby has stopped her
parents from loving her, Yoshiko goes to live among the cranes,
whose magic transforms her into one of their young for a while.
ISBN 0-531-05485-3
[1. Fairy tales. 2. Cranes (Birds) — Fiction. 3. Japan. — Fiction.
4. Babies — Fiction. 5. Brothers and sisters — Fiction.] I Title.
PZ8.C368Cr 1993 [E] — dc20 92-50843

For Alex, Matt, and Sam

Yoshiko lived with her parents in a village by the sea. In the mornings, she went for walks with her mother and found pretty pebbles on the beach.

In the evenings, she played with her father when he returned home from fishing. Soon there would be someone else to play with. Yoshiko's mother was going to have a baby.

It was exciting when the new baby arrived. He was tiny and soft and smelled like morning after the rain. Yoshiko's father named him Katsumi, and everybody loved him.

But now there were fewer walks with mother. All day
long she was bathing and feeding the baby. Now there
was not as much playing with father. He wanted to play
with Katsumi too. Yoshiko began to think her parents no
longer loved her.

The day her parents gave Katsumi his omamori amulet to protect him from evil spirits, Yoshiko was jealous. It was made from the same cloth and had the same designs as the omamori they had given her. Now she was certain she wasn't special anymore.

Yoshiko became more and more unhappy. She wanted to be a baby again. She was sure her parents wouldn't even notice if she went away. So Yoshiko walked through the misty morning toward the sea.

At the beach, she saw fish playing in the rippling water.
Pishan, pishan, the fish splashed.

"Could I be one of you?" Yoshiko asked them. "Then I could be your baby and bathe with you. Then I would be happy." But the fish didn't answer, so she walked further.

In the forest, she saw monkeys swinging in the sunlit branches. *Kii, kii,* the monkeys chattered.

"Could I be one of you?" Yoshiko asked them. "Then I could be your baby and eat nuts with you. Then I would be happy." But the monkeys didn't answer, so she walked further.

On the hilltop, she saw a flock of dancing cranes.
Cur-lew, cur-lew, the cranes cried.

"Could I be one of you?" Yoshiko asked them. "Then I could be your baby and dance with you. Then I would be happy." But Yoshiko was so tired from walking that, before the cranes could answer, she fell asleep in the tall, cool grass.

The cranes took pity on her, for she was such a lonely child.

"So be it!" said the leader. And together they swooped and whirled around her in a magical moonlit dance.

When Yoshiko awoke the next morning, she was a baby crane. All that remained of her human life was the omamori amulet her parents had placed around her neck for luck.

The cranes treated her like one of their own. They took her for walks and played with her and fed her mayflies with their beaks. As she grew older, they taught her how it was to fly, and they taught her to dance.

Yoshiko stayed with the cranes, and the seasons passed. But whenever she soared over the village by the sea, she remembered her family and wondered how they were.

Then one day Yoshiko decided to find out. She flew to her parents' house and perched high on a tree in the garden. There she overheard her mother and father telling a sad story to Katsumi.

It was about their precious first-born child, their beloved daughter, Yoshiko, and how they missed her.

Katsumi sighed and wished he had a sister to play with.

When Yoshiko saw how much her parents worried and how Katsumi needed a playmate, she wanted to be a girl again.

Cur-lew, cur-lew, she called, but they didn't understand.
She leapt into the air and swooped to the ground. She
bowed and stretched her wings.

She began to dance to show them she was well, but still they didn't recognize her. Tears sprang to her eyes. She whirled round and round until she was dizzy.

She jumped so high that she caught her wing on a branch and tore it badly. Then, hurt and exhausted, Yoshiko fainted and crumpled to the ground.

When Yoshiko opened her eyes, her family was leaning over her. Katsumi fanned her with a branch. Her mother tended the wounded wing while her father dripped cool water into her beak. Happiness filled her heart. For the first time in a long while, Yoshiko felt truly loved again.

As her mother gently stroked Yoshiko's feathers, her fingers closed around something familiar. A look of wonder appeared on her face. It was Yoshiko's omamori!

"Yoshiko?" she whispered.

At the sound of her name, the magic of the cranes ended, and Yoshiko became a girl again. Her parents were overjoyed to have her home, and she finally understood they had never stopped loving her.

In the days that followed, Yoshiko heard the cranes
calling, *Cur-lew, cur-lew*. And when she did, she would
touch her omamori and remember how it was to fly.

Then she and Katsumi would dance together under the sky, to show the cranes she was happy.

The Crane

The crane is a well-loved bird that has been depicted in Chinese and Japanese art through the ages. Its beauty and elegance alone are reason enough for the crane's popularity. But this bird has also become a symbol of long life and parental love.

Cranes are attentive parents. They will fuss over a weak chick, keeping it warm and taking great care that stronger infants don't snap all the food away from it. If in spite of such devotion a chick dies, the parents will scream loudly for several hours and be reluctant to leave it until they are sure nothing can revive it. It's little wonder that the cranes in this story took pity on Yoshiko and sheltered her for a while.

From ancient times, cranes were kept by Chinese emperors and lords. The custom spread to Japan, and even today these elegant birds are prized as pampered, living ornaments in many gardens.

The Omamori

Omamori are good luck charms thought to bring good health, safety, and financial success. Though usually made of paper or wood, some, like Yoshiko's, are made of cloth. Omamori are sold by priests at Shinto shrines and Buddhist temples. They are placed in family altars, doorways, fields, vehicles, or any place where extra protection might be desired. Omamori are also carried or worn about the neck as a more personal form of insurance against misfortune.

The Dōsojin

Stone roadside images known as dōsojin are commonly found in Japan. They are believed to be guardians of the roads and village boundaries, and the special favorites of these gods are children. Dōsojin are often dressed in bibs by worshipers, and children honor them every January in a special celebration. Perhaps the dōsojin in the illustration was keeping a close eye on Yoshiko the day she left her village.